Curious George®

A Winter's Nap

**Adaptation by Marcy Goldberg Sacks
and Priya Giri Desai
Based on the TV series teleplay
written by Craig Miller**

SCHOLASTIC INC.
New York Toronto London Auckland
Sydney Mexico City New Delhi Hong Kong

ISBN 978-0-545-43889-6

Copyright © 2010 by Universal Studios. Curious George and related characters, created by Margret and H. A. Rey, are copyrighted and trademarked by Houghton Mifflin Harcourt Publishing Company and used under license. All rights reserved. Published by Scholastic Inc., 557 Broadway, New York, NY 10012, by arrangement with Houghton Mifflin Harcourt Publishing Company. Green Light Readers and its logo are trademarks of Houghton Mifflin Harcourt Publishing Company. SCHOLASTIC and associated logos are trademarks and/or registered trademarks of Scholastic Inc.

12 11 10 9 8 7 6 5 4 3 2 1   11 12 13 14 15 16/0

Printed in the U.S.A.   40

First Scholastic printing, December 2011

Design by Afsoon Razavi and Marcy Goldberg Sacks

One fall day, Bill and George
went fishing.
Bill saw George shivering.
Maybe it was too cold to fish.

On the way home, Bill told George that some animals, such as bears, go to sleep when it gets cold. They eat a lot in the fall.

Then they hibernate,
or sleep, almost all winter. George was
curious. If he hibernated, he would
miss the cold winter months.

At home,
George ate and ate.
Maybe he would get sleepy and
hibernate.

Upstairs in bed, George tried to sleep.
But his room was too bright.

George closed
the curtains.
He painted a picture of the night sky.

He still could not sleep.
How did bears do it?

George asked the man with the yellow hat about hibernation. "This book says bears sleep in dark, quiet caves," said the man. That was it!
George needed a cave.

George hung toy bats.
He put rocks in his bed.
Now his room looked like a cave.

George settled in for his long
winter nap.

Uh-oh. Now what?
George could hear sounds outside.

Pigs oinked. Cows mooed.
Chickens clucked.
George shushed them, but they
would not be quiet.

George
covered his ears.
The animals were not as loud.
But his room was not silent yet.

George taped his blanket over
the window.
Now it was dark and quiet.

Finally, George fell asleep.
He slept in his monkey cave just
like a bear.

After a long time, George woke up.
He had done it!
He had hibernated.

"How did you sleep last night?"
asked the man.
Last night! George had slept only
one night, not all winter?
George was sad.
Then the man had an idea.
He took out a box of winter things.

The man reminded George how fun
winter was. They could sled and ski
together.
George did not want to miss winter
after all!

The Big Snooze

When animals hibernate in winter, they sleep at a time when it might be hard for them to find food. In the fall, they start to eat lots of food to store fat. Then they rest all winter long to save energy. They wake up in the spring, ready for a new season.

Bears sleep most of the winter. There are other animals that hibernate all winter long and don't wake up at all until spring.

Can you guess which animals listed include species that hibernate?

	YES	NO
BEAR	X	
LADYBUG		
CAT		
BAT		
FROG		
COW		
PIG		
GOPHER		
SQUIRREL		
SKUNK		
MONKEY		

YES ANSWERS: ladybug, bat, some frogs, some gophers, some squirrels, and some skunks

Make a Teddy Bear Cave

Put your favorite teddy bear or doll to sleep for the winter. With a few objects from inside and outside your house, you can make a cave that is comfortable to hibernate in all winter long.

1. Gather materials:

- A piece of cardboard for the floor of the cave.
- A brown paper bag to create the cave walls.
- A napkin to tuck your bear in.
- Twigs, moss, rocks, and pine needles to make the bed.
- Paints, markers, cotton balls, and anything else you need for decorating.
- A stapler.

2. Construct your cave:

- Crumple the paper bag so that you can bend it to make the cave walls and ceiling.
- With a grownup's help, staple the bag to the cardboard base. Make sure the entrance is large enough to fit your toy.
- Make the bed using the natural objects you found outside.

3. Decorate your cave like George did:

- Paint or draw bats on the cave walls.
- Place small rocks around the bed.
- Glue cotton balls around the cave to look like snow.

4. Now tuck your toy in for his own winter nap!